Letter to Aisha

and

Other Stories

Dike Okoro

Publisher's information, address:
Cissus World Press, P.O. Box 240865, Milwaukee, WI 53224
www.cissusworldpressbooks.com

ISBN: 978-0-9679511-5-7
First published in the U.S.A by Cissus World Press

Cover art: Dike Okoro

CISSUS WORLD PRESS BOOKS are published by Dike Okoro, Founding Publisher.

To God who taught me the wonders of His hands
To Chinwe for your love and support
To Mma and Uzor for your daily inspiration
To my family and friends for their encouragement

"What is life but the solving of problems from birth to death?"

--Ken Saro-Wiwa

CONTENTS

CHAPTER ONE

***

Letter to Aisha

Sister, as the sun sets this way and night becomes yet another company

inspiring nostalgia, I have decided to write to you again. Not a long letter,

but a short one; perhaps to relive our times together in a series of warm-

hearted anecdotes. The kinds you've known me for all these years. To

recoup from a generous reverie my fondest memories of our youthful days.

I know these days you are probably still wishing you could get over it all.

The hangovers from being the diplomat's wife. Take heart. Life never

settles for a fair score with anyone. I remember even you told me that.

Many, many years ago. So, today as you face the mirror and search for a

spot to place a finger, I ask that you take solace in the joy of the moment.

Your husband is a good man. He chose a profession that gives him joy.

And I know he loves you much. His absence at home for almost six

months out of a year is excusable. After all, we used to pledge to ourselves

in primary school how we looked forward to marriages that afforded us the
freedom to travel the world and know places we only visited in books and
news stories. The tall tales enriching the wives' tale. Well, you have no
excuse now. As far as I know, you live the dreams of many like me. The
friends you grew up with and with whom you tasted the often bitter waters
of being a young woman.

Do you still visit your grandma, Kehinde? Bless her soul. Such wise
elderly women are rare these days. I remember how she shielded you from
your father's whip when we were caught coming back from a late night
end of year party in secondary school. The smudge in our story book I look
at these days and smile. Especially remembering we painted our eyelashes
and lips, and pounced on the asphalt with high heels we borrowed from the
big girls on campus. How frightened you were shivering in her arms, I
remember. Those shriveled arms that covered you like the protective wings
of a hen sitting on her eggs. And your distraught father? I know till this
day he probably regrets not being allowed a moment's satisfaction to allow
his cane to leave an impressionable mark on your skin. But I don't blame
him. We all loved our strong fathers. The ones who wielded the iron fist

that instilled discipline in their children. Like we are learning these days running our own homes. Being the best mothers we can be. How often I have found myself reminding my son and daughter they don't talk back at me or say a word when I am speaking. Giving them a few lessons in scolding. I remember you saying the same about Moira. That daughter of yours who is every bit whom you used to be at her age. Always listens but ends up doing what pleases her mind. A case of self-satisfaction I see each time I remember our teenage years.

But let us be thankful to ageing. Idris is a good man. Our country is proud of him. Gone are the days when he used to sing the Pro Africanist anthem of Africa for Africans. I guess his stay in the Colombian landscape has imposed on him the many facets of cultures quilted in the exotic fabric of Latin America. I remember the love letters he shared with you which you sent my way. Cherish them all, I remember reminding you. And never give way to grudges in your heart. As for the love child's saga, I will keep praying for you. As you may know, life throws its surprises at us sometimes. And the good thing about it is not one's immediate reaction but how one handles one's self in the middle of the storm. He needed his moment to be what you had not known him to be. Now is your time to regroup after learning a part of him which I suppose shall remain a mystery to you.

You know, talking of mysteries, my daughter's sudden transformation into a lady, even though she is barely sixteen, keeps me praying for her every day she comes home to feed my perking ears bits and pieces of the same adolescent trials we once overcame as young women. How can I forget Mrs. Briggs and Mr. Amoatey, our committed grammarians at Federal Government Girls Secondary College, whose dexterity, wit, and penchant for William Shakespeare and Chinua Achebe's *Things Fall Apart* saturated our minds with dreams we only spoke about to prolong our infatuation with growing up and leaving a legacy worth emulating for our own children. I remember vividly how you stood up, declaring yourself the class prefect, even when no one had appointed you, on that day of our first class meeting for Biology, and I, to prove your temerity of heart subordinate to mine, also stood up to declare myself the class prefect. A brief exchange of harsh words soon turned both young girls, burning with the spirit of leadership, into the bosom friends we are today. Many time I have told this story to my daughter, Nkem, and she had always smiled a short one. A reassurance of sorts of what she never said but agreed seconds later, saying, "Mom, you and Aunty Aisha must have been destined for friendship even before you met in school."

And do I fault my daughter for her logic? Never. It takes a true daughter to read a mother's steps. The same way we read our mothers' and grandmothers' steps. Not to forget, our fathers too! Or have you forgotten so quickly that we come from a tradition of proud mothers and inconsolable fathers? Our mothers were often branded mysterious because they kept secrets they sometimes took to their graves, not because they hated their husbands, but because there is liberty in keeping to oneself what one desires to be kept from the ears of the marketplace. Your paternal grandfather, I still remember, was so loved by your grandmother that she could stand in the way of a bullet aiming for his heart. Weird, isn't it? Can we easily forget her words at his burial day, an advice, perhaps, that it takes a forgiving wife to love a husband who falters while striving to be a good father to his children? Responsibilities. Such an unstoppable wheel it is while heading down a slope.

11

Dear, I have been writing since 9 o'clock and the necessity to carry on has been all this heart proffers to the generous muse. Therefore, to our priceless friendship I owe this effusive outpour. Have I told you I once boarded a Flight headed for Chicago from Lagos with Chibuzor Chukwuma? Yes, the lad we branded 'Mathematician' during our holiday classes at the School of Basic Studies, Port Harcourt. What a committed Medical Practitioner he has turned into presently, one that reminded me of an ambitious dream to build a clinic in his hometown. Such aspiration in a young man who used to hand you the love letters his young heart couldn't keep from pouring onto pages, to hand to me even while we both sat at the base of the mango tree in the front yard of my family home. Dear, memories! Can a pounding heart ever do without them? Do you remember Ibinabo and Onyeka? I crossed paths with them one Saturday morning in Harrods in London while traveling to Italy with Sarah last June. An arranged meeting at Brompton Road, I supposed at the time. They both send their greetings to you and still find it hard to believe you married Idris. Well, your father's strong arms must have done the miracle. Like mine I suppose. How preposterous it is these days to look at our childhood and pretend the hand of God of wasn't working overtime on our destinies. You the imam's daughter and I the pastor's daughter.

On several occasions I have replayed our roles as stubborn children and thanked whatever spirits guided us thus for not allowing us to stoop so low as to accept what we had not wholeheartedly believed. Musa, O Musa. How you loved him and yet lost him in the end. Through it all I stood by you, our faces both covered with hijab. So bizarre the scene. I was there when you both professed your undying love for each other under the guava tree. His was amplified through wondrous acts. The swimmer from Kano. Envy of all the boys from Port Harcourt and far across Rivers State. He swam like a fish. Feet flapping and legs appearing glued to each other as he shot ahead in water. How many medals he won at the state championships I do not remember. But I do remember the one day he tried a flip from the board and ended up floating in a pool of his own blood, having crushed the back of his head on the edge of the swimming pool. "You will never weep this way again, not in my lifetime," I remember your grandma saying, with your face buried in my chest. Ah, Musa. Tall, lanky and handsome. When he walked through gatherings in school, his shirt flying, his collar standing, and his khaki trousers neatly ironed to match his polished sandals. And it helped he spoke such good English. Always quoting Shakespeare to dish out a dint of wisdom every now and then. Such model for a young man. May our daughters find them these days without having to weep later like we used to. And every so often I have seen his face appear in the mind's mirror, even after twenty five years, only to blot it out with a smile and say to myself, without words, the years of our childhood: can they ever be forgotten? Yesterday it was you and Musa. Today Idris has taken his place. A tree rooted to the soil of the land, I must say. I remember the first time he flew alone to Bogota and then a few weeks later you received these very lines, a somber afterthought from the Chilean Nobel Prize for Literature poet's poem, "Tonight I Can Write the Saddest Lines": "Love is so short, forgetting is so long." Have we not lived through this all our lives, dearest?

My father scolded me for fasting along with you in observance of the Ramadan. Poor old man. What did he know about girls and relationships? Our journeys in life are more than butterflies settling on flowers. Our bonds are like threads on fabric. Hardly at war, unless the

14

intoxicating envy creeps in to torment the mind. Eid-Al-Fitr shaped us in its own way, even though I professed to you quite often the relevance of Easter and Christmas. Yet we never allowed our confessions of knowing God in our own trained ways to turn our relationship into two roads that met and fought over which was deserving of utmost respect. You schooled me, I remember, in the mannerisms of a lady. I who grew up kicking soccer balls with boys and thinking how tough I was. Once I punched a boy in the eye and received the weirdest rebuke from the neighborhood folks, both young and old, for fear, perhaps, that they had watched a terrorist flower blossom in their midst. How wrong they were. You remember that day perfectly, don't you? After rejecting his advances he had branded me *ashawo*, the prostitute's title. One does not have to accept a title not earned, especially when there was no reward attached to it, I remember grandfather saying to me one night I stayed up late moon-watching with him and taking in all I could from the sea of wisdom. That was that! The bully himself would tender his apologies weeks later to spare me the growing murmurs of hearts who were quick to follow the rumormongering. You came a day later and stayed with me till nightfall,

15

when your cousin Danladi, that fine soccer player, the one for whom school was not meant for, like we heard him repeatedly air in protest to his parents, came to walk you home. Please, remember to tell me what has become of him. Does he too have a family like us? Or is he still plying the trade of bachelorhood? We know how busy men can be with visiting the marketplace for the hand of the perfect woman. Too bad they will never believe it is they who make it hard on themselves to make a choice. Not the other way around. It is like while they keep watch at the gates, we sing our lives by just being free like our minds. Honoring the sun when it shines our way; keeping our hearts focused when it rains.

Tomorrow I shall light a candle in the dark in celebration of the fifteenth year anniversary of my marriage to Pastor Israel Amadi. I had barely known my husband when I was reminded of an agreement between his father and mine, two pastors, to betroth their children in the future. The mere fact that we have lasted this long still baffles me. I didn't know trust and courage like I do today, especially since I once looked at our marriage like two people blindfolded and sent on a mission into a forest at night. He is the sweetest, I must say, my Israel. Not a day goes by I don't get a gift from him. Twice I asked him to stop and on countless occasions he has politely intoned that I should allow him to love me the best way he knows how. The necklaces from India, the Ankara and lace and George fabric. My closet is full and I know there's more coming. But my sister-in-law, Nonye. What a blessing she's been. Her coming always relieves my closet of the mounting gifts. And on future visits I have heard her brother, my own husband, declare with unquestionable surety, if the fabric she has on was a gift from me. And Nonye, wise beyond the person I know, dismisses her brother's speculation with the gentle, "ah, ah, brother. You don't think I can afford buying this for myself? So what do you think I have been doing with all the money sent to me while on campus?"

Israel, Israel! He learned fast and soon stopped to be steadfast in suspicion. He is doing well these days. The church is growing, and very soon we might be relocating to a new building in town. Port Harcourt has changed, but the old structures still remain. Guess the local adage old soldiers never die lives in things non-human too. The defining stopovers of our youthful days. Hotel Presidential and Catering Guest House. Harley Street and Rumuola Road sure left us quite a legacy to hold on to. The swimming pool and frequent parties after school. What do you say our visits to friends at Shell Residential Area in Rumukurushi? If Abuja had a secret paradise to charm the youths with the best modern life in the city could offer, we knew of the promise of bright dawn from the amenities at the disposal of age mates we branded Shell's children. The kids we felt belonged to the privileged class, most of whom extended our way favors beyond the reach of material acquisition. Comics. Mills and Boon. Bike rides down streets as clean as you can imagine. The latest DVDs imported. Friendships we made and left as the new dawn set us on paths requiring a shift in focus. The decisions that would shape our social lives. Look at us today: married and parents. Oftentimes I have thought about our kids and wondered if they too will climb the ladder occasionally missing steps to recognize the imperfection that is life. And my son Martins has not failed me. You tell me he is your friend and I have reminded him over and over to behave when I find him climbing the guava tree to pluck fruit instead of asking the house help, Sampson, to do the climbing for him. Only nine, he is already a handful. Quite the opposite of the child I had envisioned. Israel's late father is who he personifies in everything he does. Sometimes

I am pressed to ask where I went wrong or what I had failed to do to impose the rules from my books on him.

But aren't our children's lives sometimes mirrors of ours? Dear, do you remember our weekend shopping sprees at Leventis and Kingsway stores? The lure of imported food, clothes and shoes we pledged our allegiances to, for our generation and the finest of times under our country's leadership. These days I carry my bottled water like I do my handbag, trusting the craze to stay healthy and reminding my dear Martins to watch his daily intake of soft drinks. And I must thank his involvement in athletics at school for his adherence to my pleas. Like I keep drumming into his earlobes, every step taken in the direction of a healthy lifestyle will safe him the apprehension of visits to the physician's office in future. Sister, the tide wave certainly is a lover of change in mood swings! Do you know oftentimes I have craved the unnecessary indulgence in food habits we used to wallow in during our childhood? The Saturday morning stop at the supermarket for ice cream, defeating the purpose of our exercise routine at the athletic club, eh! But what can I say about cravings and appetite, especially when the older one gets the harder it becomes to let go of what has become customary. My son calls my concerns midlife crises and scold him without regret, to the point he apologizes for his bland remarks. We have to healthy these days, for there is nothing more betraying to the spirit than which the body not taken care of exposes to the eyes.

Dearest, don't we owe our kids more than stories of survival? It is not often one pauses to ponder how the fussing plastic bag detained by a tree branch somehow ends up wallowing in freedom. Yes, our lives, I have sometimes thought, compares to that of the fated plastic bag. Out of sorrow we have learned to seek joy in our losses. Did I write to tell you grandma Kehinde is no more? My dear grandma, the mother hen of my father's household! Yes, she is now amongst the stars that beautify the night sky. I do not say this out of a rigid religious worldview but out of a self-arrived belief I have kept close to my heart for the past twenty years. That we are one with nature. Or, as isn't the same when we are told to dust must everyone return? So you see the fulcrum of this ideation I wish to impose on you? Let us hope our kids do not look too far from nature when I puzzled about the things of the ebb and tide that dictate our daily

20

wanderings in the market of ideas. Perhaps we can find consolation in the fact that growing, for us whose footprints must serve as guides to theirs, wasn't about searching for the particulars of what made us different from our parents. Instead we accommodated the peculiarities of strings that supported us without any attachments to things negating change.

Enough about the kids and our expectations. When are you visiting? I have arranged for a short trip to Chicago, where we would spend time combing the famed Devon Avenue for jewelries and fabric from India. The finest you can find, my dear. And Saris too. Until you write back, this is wishing you and your family the best of times. May God's hands keep you safe till we meet my sister!

Moji

CHAPTER TWO

***

Mene's Song

Port Harcourt was restless that week. Reporters from Europe and the U.S. thronged the international airport at Omagwa, just a few miles from the notorious Catch-Fire Prison where the renowned environmentalist and fiction writer, Mene, had been detained for treason. His crime included his speaking up, and daring the military boys in West Africa's beehive to savor in their romance with unreported acts of genocide committed in his oil-rich hometown. And Mene, with his wealth of ideas and fame worldwide, barely escaped the last genocide that drew an unforgettable bedlam across the country and sweeping criticisms from Washington D.C. and London.

Nights in his cell were terrible. But for the roach that kept him awake occasionally, the silence was mind shattering. Sometimes he pretended to be smoking pipe and imagined himself holding his woman while they both rocked to the sultry voice of Cardinal Rex Jim Lawson's High life music at a bar, until the echoes of the warden's spikes down the hall cut short his moments of nostalgia and then he assumed his sleeping position on the concrete, with eyes wide open. The dry air within the cells did not help, either. When the heat got to him, he changed his position on the floor so he would not be denied a good sleep. Such was the daily ritual he put himself through, just to keep mind and body together. At other times, especially when it rained at night, he would imagine the letters he wrote, things he said at public rallies, and the tormenting voices he had deposited in the repository and psyche of the khaki boys who roamed the streets guzzling their ambitions in bars and priding themselves in expensive imports and brand new jeeps, boasting of ghost bank accounts in Switzerland and the US while running the affairs of a country so blessed and yet many of its bright minds, university graduates included, milled about jobless. In truth, Mene enjoyed smuggling those letters to his good friend and writing pal, Tsepho, a fearless journalist twice nominated for South Africa's version of the Pulitzer Prize for journalism, who lived in Houston, Texas. Both writers had struck a friendship while in attendance at a PEN International

Conference in Los Angeles several years ago. Back then Mene's desire to become a writer was spurred by his open rejection of all apartheid stood for in Tsepho's homeland. But with the coming and passing of new decades came sweeping changes. Tsepho's country had seen its worst days turn into promising days, and apartheid's presence had been drastically abolished by a soaring regime spearheaded by Nelson Mandela, a former political prisoner and freedom fighter turned national hero.

Yet Mene's disconsolation was not hidden. A prisoner was not what he envisaged. At least not in a country he always bragged in his writings had unlimited potentials, especially in its Niger Delta region. But prison had its own wars. Wars that broke men, left them in tears, and denied them freedom in cuffs while they sought consolation in the night stars, holding back tears to hide their shame. And Mene was one of such men. The only break he got was during the day, when sun's ray whisked through doors opened by the wardens. Then he strutted about briskly wondering or sat in bed and tried to convince himself that he was quite fortunate to have worn copies of Ngugi's *Detained: A Prison Diary* and Dostoyevsky's *Notes from the Underground* to preserve his sanity.

24

Often, with his face feeling the cold iron doors and his hands firmly holding the iron dividers, he enjoyed a good laugh as fellow prisoners sang from their cells, "Since e-morning *e-yo*. We never eat o, *e-yo*."

Their guttural voices gave him hope, hope the kind he knew he could never be assured, as long as he remained separated from the society and family he cherished unconditionally. Occasionally, when a prisoner delivered a salvo of farts or belched repeatedly, he would laugh aloud and later join in the chorus of thanks givers who would chant "Well done-o!" from their cells. Such moments reminded him of the humanity all those incarcerated shared. But time always had its own way of executing betrayal. Two hours ago, behind closed doors and amid the specter of a heated debate in the capital city of Abuja, Mene's execution by hanging had been mandated by the president, a pot-bellied army general whose distaste for writers had never been in doubt.

"Smoke the bastard! I don't care if America breathes down our neck or if the British instigate our expulsion from the commonwealth council. They'll always come back to trade on oil with us. Enough for the writing bastard! Let's see how he's going to conjure more provocative words to fuel his delight when the rope is around his neck!"

The aftermath of the meeting sent jitters down the spine of reporters and educators. There was the fear of a mass riot in Port Harcourt, birthplace and hometown of the detained activist and writer. Schools were closed. Students abandoned their rooms in campuses and headed home. All calls to the president from Washington D.C. and London were not returned. Mene's fate had been decided.

On the night of his execution, strange happenings occurred to alert him of what lay ahead. He returned from the day's manual labor of cleaning the latrine and cutting the grass outside to discover his treasured books missing. His attempt to make a formal complaint was denied audience. The cockroach that kept him hopeful like a burning lamp was a no show. The warden who took bribes from him to deliver his written notes to his journalist pal was conspicuously missing in action. Mene sat on the cement floor of his cell, knees drawn close to his chest, paper on his knees, stump of pencil between his wet fingers, and laboriously printed his last written

words:

> Even in the hours
> When the call for verse
> Cheated the singer,
> The cry for the homeland
> Remained his song.

CHAPTER THREE
***

The Cross Bearer

I had just finished devouring a meal of pounded yam and egusi soup one afternoon at a cheap buka off the Expressway in Port Harcourt when a short man stormed the buka with two armed police officers. Without hesitation, he pointed at me and said: "There he is, the coward who impregnated my daughter! Arrest him!" Alarmed, I dipped my hands in the hand wash bowl of water and afterwards attempted to make a dash for the door, but the officers struck me on the head with their batons. I lost control of my legs, fell backwards and hit the back of my head on a solid wood. When I regained consciousness I was sitting on the floor of a crowded and noisy police station. Every corner of the station was swarmed with complaints. People brought roosters and goats recovered from armed robbers and filed charges of petty robbery. The officers on desk duty collected evidences presented and scribbled down notes feverishly onto their little pad. A bit dazed and not fully awake, I gazed at the officers faces hoping to find a helper. My luck, as it appeared, seemed to be running out. I soon realized I had witnessed these scenes before in my imagination when friends who had been arrested poured over their dreadful experiences in anecdotes. When I looked behind me I saw a long bench placed against the wall. Shoes, bags, and other personal items yet to be inspected and documented were stacked on it. I went over and sat there, combing my thoughts as I waited for my turn to be attended to.

After a short while an irritated voice cursed from the cell behind the front desk: "Stupid officers! God go punish all of una for not giving us food this afternoon!" Another voice with a measure of anger added: "Officers, I wan shit o!" More and more insults and complaints piled up from the cell. The afternoon dragged on. The heat in the station exacerbated. I was soon handed a paper and ordered to write down my name, address, phone number and details of the crime that led to my arrest. I drew close to the attending officer and told him I didn't understand why I had been arrested in the first place. "Look here, young man, I am not here to play games with you. State exactly when and where you met the girl, and what happened before your arrest," he replied. A neatly dressed man with a breath smelling of roasted peanut, he had spoken softly without looking me in the face. Drooping over the desk, I conjured up a chain of events unrelated to the accusation leveled against me and put them in a summary. Soon came the lead officer, a tall and lanky man with glasses resting on top of his nose. He snatched the paper from my hand, cleaned up the groundnut shells on his desk and said: "Stupid boy!"

I spent a very long time standing there and figuring what next was going to happen. I knew if I went into the cell that afternoon I was going to face a terrible ordeal. Nigerians who ended up on the bad notes of mean police officers at police stations such as the one I was detained at knew they were likely to be exposed to all forms of abuse and weird cellmates once put in a cell. At a point in time I was miffed as I mulled over the possible reasons my good friend Furo, with whom I had gone to the buka to eat before my arrest had not turned up to bail me. I was thirsty and there was little to no possibility of drinking water being made available.

"Swallow your spit as water," I had heard an officer say when an inmate cried for water. Apprehension overtook me, driving home the message. I was doomed. Furo had not interfered with the officers when they whisked me off. I didn't blame him for I knew he couldn't take the risk of being put in cuffs as an accomplice to an alleged crime. The more I thought he should have done something to help avert my predicament, the more it occurred to me that he probably had not apprised my boss, an army colonel, of my whereabouts. I closed my eyes and thought of the short man, his sudden rage and the blank expression on his face after dishing his orders to the officers. Then I began to worry. Was I the victim of a hoax? Images of the scene at the buka shortly before my arrest flashed through my mind. I remembered vividly how a man eating ravenously in the same buka had said to a friend over the phone that he was rushing out of town because a certain rich man's daughter had claimed he got her pregnant. Suddenly the man's face became apparent in my mind. I could see his dimples and bloodshot eyes. He had on a face cap which he pulled to the side of his face rakishly. A flurry of reasons as to why he probably wasn't arrested raced through my mind. When I got tired of recollecting the

distressing events I sat on the floor and yawned. Then I fell asleep.

When I woke up my trouser and shirt and shoes were lying on the
ground next to me.

"Young man, you are lucky!" said an officer standing behind the desk.

"Get up," he ordered. I stood and wobbled. "Stand straight," he added. I

saw him turn round and hand blank note sheets to two men brought to the

station on handcuffs, ordering them to sit on the floor next to me.

"Criminals! Look at your faces! Don't worry. You will tell your stories to

your cell mates." One of the men had on a face cap which he pulled to the

side of his face rakishly. When our eyes met he quickly put his head down.

I stared at him and began to imagine the scenes at the buka before my

arrest. In my mind I heard the man's voice while he chatted over the phone.

A sudden burst of anger swelled in me. But with the attending officer

holding my trouser and shirt up in the air, waving them, I wasted no time

in sidling up to the desk. After putting on my clothes, I was given a

notebook to sign off for the personal items returned. I think it was after

signing and placing the pen in the middle of the notebook that it first occurred to me that my wristwatch had not been given to me. I waited for the officer to close the notebook. When turned around I noticed the look of suspicion in his eyes, but summoned enough courage to tell him my wristwatch had not been returned.

'What is happening to this one? You are given a free ride to go home and you are hear crying over a stupid watch, eh! I see you like it here already."

'No, no, officer,' I said.

'Good,' said the officer.

As soon as I got outside I noticed more people arrested were being brought to the station for booking and detention. I didn't bother about looking at their faces. I ventured down the road exhilarated at the liberty I had earned. My head ached with pains. I went to a shed across the road and sat down on a bench. A weak breeze whiffed past and as I was about to pay for a soft drink the woman selling the foot items at the shed told me someone had already paid. When I asked who, she pointed at a Peugeot 504 across the road. Furo wound down the window and waved at me. "Don't be in a hurry," he shouted. "Take your time." I took a sip of the Coca Cola and, imprisoned by silence, wondered what was going on. But there were no readily available answers for me. It was only in the morning of the following day that I felt better knowing that my good friend had done his best to get me out of detention that was undeserving. My boss had been alerted by Furo and through his call for a thorough investigation the short man had been outmuscled by powers greater than his and more connected, to the point that he feared the worst and ordered for my release, for his daughter had identified the culprit with photo evidence who was eventually arrested.

CHAPTER FOUR

***

A Generous Gift

So strange, so daring was her figure in the dark that night she walked down the empty road alone looking like one possessed by a deranged spirit. Nobody knew why or understood the point of it all. At a point she stopped, gazed studiously at the sky as though speaking to an imaginary being and then resumed her aimless walk. She had not been walking to any place in particular. Perhaps her intentions had made no sense, for just when she got to end of the road she turned around and started off to the opposite direction.

Npisi watched from under the canopy of the bar overlooking the road, his eyes stalking the shadowy figure as he waited to be served his order of pepper soup and Guilder beer. The television placed on the table by the door beside his chair relayed the night news. A transistor radio set on top of the TV played Fela's *Coffin for Head of State*. A group of four men occupying the table behind Npisi laughed hysterically, arguing about the woman.

"Ah, that one nah witch. Abi you sef no see how she dey look?" said one of the men. "Come on, take it easy. A fine girl like that? I have seen her face in daylight. She can't be no witch. Probably dealing with her own wahala, like we all do sometimes, you know!" added another.

Irritated by the jibes directed at the strange woman, Npisi shook his head, washed his hands, paid for his orders and left the bar. As he strode toward the road, he foraged his mind for words.

He had decided he was going to have a chat with her.

The night got cold and he soon discovered he was standing behind her. How he got beside her sooner than he had anticipated was beyond him. He cleared his throat.

"Cold night, eh," he said.

She turned around and smiled broadly.

"So why are you out here alone," he enquired.

She was hesitant to speak. A coy expression glowed in her eyes.

"I am visiting town for the first time and my aunt who was supposed to be my host had traveled before I got to her home."

"Oh dear, e-yaaa!" exclaimed Npisi. "That is rather unfortunate, but I can house you for the night if you wouldn't mind."

"You?" she intoned suspiciously. "Abeg me I no be ashawo o!" she retorted.

"Haba, tufiakwa!" exclaimed Npisi. "You must don't think there are no good men left in this world, eh," he added.

For the first that night Npisi noted something about her that had won him over. Her soft voice and youthful countenance had suddenly rubbed off on him in an endearing way. Wasting no time, he waved to a stop a taxi and hopped in after her. They had not spoken to each other for the rest of the drive until they got to his one bed room apartment at O village in the city. Instead they smiled at each other whenever a congestion in traffic delayed the driver. Npisi felt lucky. In his mind he was grateful he had summoned up courage to speak to her. "Wow, it was good I completely ignored those drunk men vomiting gibberish about her," he said to himself. "Who knows, maybe they've made advances towards her which she had turned down to their distaste," he contended silently. By this time the driver's music system was playing "This world is not my home," by Jim Reeves. Then the rusty Datsun went past the last light and stopped by the gutter overlooking a bush.

Npisi reached for the front pocket of his shirt and counted some money which he handed to the driver.

"Are we there yet?" asked the lady sheepishly.

"Yes my dear," said Npisi, elation gathering in his eyes.

They could hear the loud chants of crickets and the mounting croaking of frogs. From where they stood buildings with lights shone at a distance. They had to walk through the bush, quietly pushing toward his apartment. Somehow, in a sudden wave of unexplainable feeling, Npisi became feverish. His head ached and he stopped, feeling his forehead with his palms.

"Are you okay?" asked the lady.

"Fine, am fine," he said.

Soon they got to his place. The neighbors seating outside, a man and a woman, greeted Npisi. He nodded and faced his door. Then he pulled out his key from his trouser pocket, opened the door and let her go in first.

Standing inside his apartment he could feel his feverish condition getting

worse. So he tore open a packet of Panadol, swallowed two tablets and

drank a cup of water. All the while she stood by the door, watching him.

Npisi heard the cry of a cat and stared at the window open-eyed. "Did you

hear that?"

"What?" she asked.

"I could swear I heard a cat cry!" he said.

She smiled and said: "You need to lay in bed. You've had a long day."
He sat still by this time. She came over, helped him take off his shirt and

shoes, and then assisted him in lying on his back. He stayed silent, gazing

into her eyes that now glowed. For a moment fear engulfed him, but he felt

reassured as she adjusted the pillow under his head. Then he pointed

frantically at the door, asking her to make sure it was locked, for armed

robbers were known to be on rampage in the area at night, sniffing like

dogs at every opportunity to profit from the ordinary citizen. As she

walked to the door for the first time that night he noticed she walked

barefoot and that her heels barely touched the ground. A distorted view overtook his mind and he felt like getting down from bed. But, like a

trance, she was already standing by him by the time he sought to throw a

leg down from bed.

"Relax," she said.

He looked at her, his heart beating fast.

"What seems to be the matter? You don't want me to stay?" she asked, her

hand rubbing his chest gently.

"Oh no," he said. "Please help me cover my feet with the bed sheet. Am

kind of cold." As she bent towards his feet he noticed a scar on the side

of her face and swallowed hard. Then she joined him in bed and set the

lantern on the table by his pillow. They both were silent. Soon they fell

asleep. His snoring was loud. Every now and then he opened his eyes and

looked her way and their eyes met. He smiled, closed his eyes and went

back to sleeping. Later that night when he woke up the lantern had lost its

light and it was very dark. He tried to get down from bed but stopped the

moment he heard a woman's voice ask: "What do you think you're

doing?" He turned to look at the direction from where the voice came but

couldn't see her face. Then his fear transformed into a wave of confidence. Then he started touching her body, feeling her from the top

to the bottom.

"Do you know what you're doing" the woman asked.

"Yes," he whispered.

She was still. A sudden wave of silence crowded the room, even though

outside it was windy. Again he heard the cat crying. The photographs on

the wall fell down, shattering. He was sure that was what had happened but

couldn't get down to verify for himself. Soon a stench that was unbearable

overtook the room. Below his back he felt something crawl out and drop to

the floor. The last thing he noticed was that he had started experiencing a

faint spell. Then he lost consciousness.

When he woke up later the lantern was still burning and the room

was bright. He stared about in disbelief. Holding his head, he rolled down

from bed and stood still for a while. A moment later he noticed there was

water on the floor. It looked as though it had rained at night and the roof

had leaked. He went by the window and pulled aside the curtain. The

rising sun cut through the window, adding more light to the room. Then

the astonishing discovery hit him. He was alone in the room. There was no trace of the lady that accompanied him home last night. His room smelled

of incense. He had never liked incense and could not grasp how or why the

burnt incense got to his room. Instantly worries had set in on his mind. His

cellphone had been buzzing and he had not paid any attention to it. He

yawned, stretched his arms and picked up the cellphone. Then he listened

to his missed messages. He had been sacked from his job and had been

told to stop by the week after to pick up his severance pay. A sad

expression took over his face. As though that was not enough the next

message got him mad. "Brother hurry, hurry, papa is dying. We are all at

BM hospital." The last message was from his personal physician, who

wished to meet with him urgently to go over the results of his latest blood

test for HIV.

Galvanized, Npisi sat on the waterlogged floor, silent. His lips moved but
not a word was

uttered. Uncertainty sat on his mind, corroborating with the sudden

helplessness which had taken over him.

Meanwhile, in a bush across the road facing the bar where he ate

pepper soup and drank his beer the night before, an old woman with her back facing the son, poured a reddish liquid over the head of a prostrating lady. "You have done well my daughter," said the old woman. "Now you can go out to the world and fetch me more men willing to trade their bodies for their destiny. Lust is a starving spirit. Feed it well my child. And I will never run dry of blessings for you." The old woman laughed aloud. When she stopped laughing she ordered the lady to stand up. As she stood erect, her bright eyes glowing in the sun, her identity was revealed. Npisi cried in horror.

CHAPTER FIVE
***
Untying Knots

Many who saw the lawyer could hardly imagine him the twelve-year old orphan who stood in front of the church gate on Sundays holding a dusty plastic bowl, catarrh dripping down his nose. Now a forty-two-year old man with mustache and standing almost six feet tall, he spoke volubly and walked confidently. His eyes glowed as he spoke and his gestures displayed his free will to engage people regardless of class status in conversation. Everyone in the court room seemed to have developed a liking for his personality. They nodded when he cross examined his witnesses and murmured when his witnesses paused to ponder. This would go on for a while until the end of the court meeting. The lawyer was not popular in his home town. This unfortunate cross he had to bear was passed on to him for reasons even he had failed to comprehend. On numerous occasions he had consulted a friend who doubled as a pastor and physician for advice. And as always his good friend's answer to his dilemma proved to be the same. "Blame it on your father's family." That single sentence reply was all his friend offered. But the lawyer was not satisfied. His craved for a more believable reply, knowing he never knew his father. Not to talk of his mother. And, thus, this harsh truth about his genealogy made it all the more harder for people to take him seriously.

In fact in grade school he had fought severally and had been subjected to corporal punishment by teachers. Yes, the teachers left no room to accommodate troublemakers. Any action that curbed their antics worked. Peace must be obtained by any means necessary. This, even when school mates called the lawyer, back then a quiet and shy boy, the disturbing and derogatory "born throw away", a local expression for the English word "bastard". The words ate deep into his heart, leaving him embittered. It was perfectly okay to be called names by age mates but when it was one that carried a badge of shame concerning one's genealogy, it turned out to be somewhat of a reproachable label. But that was then. Time would pass and the young man would learn how to deal with his foulmouthed schoolmates. In the meantime, finding his biological parents preoccupied his priorities. The lawyer obtained information from every elder he was directed to, especially the ones he believed knew his mother whom he never knew. Their responses tasked him to focus exclusively on the fact that he had battles to fight in life. "But isn't that something every one faces daily?" he had retorted, one day he visited his elderly uncle. The elder, a man almost ninety six, shook his head and then slowly picked up his hand fan made of raffia leaf. Whistling to himself as he sat on the stool placed in front of his door, he spoke to the lawyer without looking him in the eyes. "The problem with the young ones like you is that you never listen. And that is why your generation is besieged with so much confusion." Immediately the lawyer flew into a rage, picked up his briefcase and stood up to leave. "Sit down," said the elder. He smiled a lot and gently picked on pieces of kola nut placed on a saucer by his feet. The lawyer had no choice. He was the one who came seeking information.

The elder was a popular face in the village of Odu. Admired by all for his elocution, he had not attended school or had any formal education but could read perfectly and appeared to be knowledgeable beyond expectation. Rumor had it that he had worked as a court clerk for the British prior the Nigeria's independence. Hence the probable reason for his articulate command of English. In church on Sundays, the same elder took to the pulpit to read prescribed books and verses of the Bible to the amazement of an attentive congregation. His diction, an obvious part of his likable personality, earned him respect from family and strangers. Remembering the old man's eloquence in church now, the lawyer sat down and listened as the elder began to speak. It seemed a mirror of life suddenly opened from the old man's wrinkled face and deep eyes. His voice, though soft, audibly relayed his carefully chosen words, taking the lawyer to times when the village was pristine, beautified by the love story of an elementary school teacher and a youth corper who had served the same elementary school in the capacity of teacher. It was a time when professionalism was shown the door and courtship earned men favors. Michael, as the teacher was known, was the perfect man. Standing six feet tall and brawny, he spoke with a deep voice that endeared him to women. His students honored him with obedience. It was the much they could offer in appreciation for strict approach to teaching. After all, they prided in the fact that they were rewarded with his knowledge, the very gift that endeared him to

Clementina the youth corper from the city, a lady whose charm attracted men of all ages.

When school was over for the day he waited for her by her classroom and walked her home. Students warmed up to the duo, even accompanying them often. They would hold hands, smile at each other and stop over at roadside roasts to buy roasted plantain and mackerel. Their union seemed the fairy tale bliss. In the village of Odu they maintained wonderful rapport with one another. The students longed for their company and when they succeeded, went home satisfied with the tutoring they received. Colleagues envied both teachers but kept a distance. The students were topmost priority. Anyone who could get their attention and make them to come to class regularly must have some God-given gifts that must be respected.

Michael was the kind of man who never complained. He took charge of his class with dignity, and loved challenging his students in ways that brought the best out of them. "Good job, good job!" colleagues would hear him say from a distance, when a student offered an answer or opinion that met his approval. But when he disapproved of answers, he never condemned students to chiding. Instead he immediately said: "That is not the answer I am looking for at this moment." Then an eerie silence took over the class. Clementina often watched from his classroom window when her class was not in session, smiling and admiring his wit and vivacity.

Michael tucked his shirts and wore starched khaki trousers to work. His major areas of teaching, History and Literature, afforded him the liberty of drawing from experience in making his lectures lively. He had been exposed to Shakespeare and the Greek classics and the quizzical narratives of Cyprian Ekwensi's *The Leopard's Claws*, Amos Tutuola's *The Palm-Wine Drinkard*, and Chinua Achebe's *Things Fall Apart*, and quite often he referenced such texts to enlighten students on the role of tragedy in modern literature or historical figures.

But there was far more about Michael and Clementina that the young lawyer needed to know. The elder paused, blew his nose hard and wiped his hands on his wrapper. Then he cleared his throat and began talking. The young lawyer watched with the attentiveness of a cat tracking a mouse, waiting patiently for the end to the old man's tale. The same tale he had been made to believe might lead to the end of the riddle that his life had become. Michael was my son by a woman I once met at Apapa in Lagos, started the elder. His voice becoming emotional, he shook his head and stopped speaking. "You must leave now," he said, but the resolute young lawyer insisted he carry on with his story. "Yes, go on. So what happened?" The elder hesitated for a moment, shrugged and retraced the day he came home from work tired and met Michael and Clementina in the living room. They had been waiting for him. There was nothing between them that gave away the indication that they had come to seek his blessing for their proposed marriage. To him, the meeting was just like any other he would expect a young man of Michael's age who, finding a young woman's attracted and worthy of being made his wife, had initiated a formal introduction to a parent. He welcomed the idea with great pleasure and offered the young couple Fanta and chin chin. They ate and thanked him. Then they fed their eyes on his album and left before it got dark outside. Two days later an old friend from Odu village, a primary school teacher who used to live with the elder as a maid but left after she intimated her pregnancy for him, sent word through her brother to tell the elder that her daughter, his own daughter, would be getting married to a young man from

Apapa. Already overcome with shock at the possible end of the tale, the young lawyer stood up to leave. In his head many things fought for attention. He had noticed how hesitant the elder had become while he spoke. The fear he dreaded on his way to see the old man had now ambushed him. He could run to nowhere now but must face reality like a man.

"So Michael and Clementina were your own children."

"By no fault of mine, I swear, ah, God," reiterated the elder.

"And I am the baby, your grandson," the young lawyer added.

They both had many things to say to each but didn't know where to start of who would take the first initiative to break the silence. The young lawyer now believed what his friend the pastor and physician had told him about seeking answers from his father's house. Even though he never had a personal relationship with his father or mother, at least now he knew their etymology and how it related to his in a convoluted network. To know of this at forty did him more harm than good. But he would take it like a pinch of life. Every experience would serve as a learning curve, just like he always reminded his clients after a date in court. Not anymore would he seat alone at home and whine about what a mess his life had become. The choice was now perfectly his. He could start all over again. His grandfather, even at ninety six, was still there to offer an open arm. But would whatever friendship that transpired between equate that between a father and a son? Tough lines. These were the unspoken truths he kept to himself as he entered his Mercedes Benz that afternoon and drove off.

The following morning he did not go to work. There was a heavy downpour that lasted till early evening. The streets and roads were flooded. Debris from pits and gutters swarmed the open. People stayed indoors. He got down from bed and stretched to admire his muscles and then he yawned. By the time he got to his phone he had noticed the missed calls blinking.

The bad weather seemed to have foreshadowed something bad. All the calls came from the village. It was Maria, his own aunt, the elder's daughter, who left the messages. The old man had succumbed to an untimely heart attack in the early hours of the morning and had been pronounced dead. When the young lawyer called the crying and shouting in the background had left him incapacitated. "Brother, brother," cried a young lady. "Grandpa dead!" The young lawyer sat down with his phone resting on his thigh. Of all the things that would happen to him in the rest of the year and the years to come, he only regretted his not being able to have a fatherson relationship with his grandfather, the elder. So unreasonable of him, he would recall, not to have asked for pictures of Michael and Clementina. But time, like many would concede, healed wounds. This he would recall six years later, sitting in his porch, observing his wife pushing their son in his tricycle, while he, holding Clementina's faded photo, says to himself, "God, mother was so extraordinarily beautiful."

CHAPTER SIX
***

That "Amen"

My neighbor Ndu was rushed to the hospital this afternoon. What happened I asked anxiously?

His young wife who sat on the porch, arms folded, would not say a word. Not to me. Not to any stranger however sympathetic. She sat there loosening her braids, chewing on gum, and staring at the ostentatious photos of half-naked models featured in the torn pages of the *Vogue* fashion magazine she placed on her laps. Nobody dared to ask her why she did not follow the ambulance that vanished with a cacophony of sirens. Instead whispers soared and died until the crowd that had gathered dispersed.

I stood there, staring at her until I accepted my reluctance to be a party to the calamity that had befallen the celebrated couple who lived next door to my wife and me. Then I walked into my one bedroom flat and shut the door.

"AMEN".

That was the word that slipped out of my mouth, with my eyes closed. Whether I meant what I said did not matter to me. My utterance was genuine, and that was all that mattered.

Before Ndu was rushed to a hospital in a Good Samaritan's rusty, old Totoya Celica that afternoon, I had never, all my life, wished evil on anyone. Not even those I considered enemies. But his was a different case altogether. His story troubled me like a fly stalking a wounded dog. A pest! That was what he was to me. Because of him I have been married three times. And all three ex- wives of mine, ungrateful to my show of kindness and financial support, had accused me of stinginess, and that I never cared about their upkeep.

"Were we e worun la ubachi e wurun!"

Those were the harsh words of the last of them, Ada, before she slammed the door to my face. I sure needed no one to remind me that when we left the world we did not carry with us our wealth or riches.

Hell, I was not rich, but I knew how to save money. But Ndu, oh Ndu, that conniving wretch, brought me more pain than I could imagine. Every day he came back from work produced a night of fussing and fighting at my home. My wife would taunt me from one corner of the living-room to the other. With my fingers gripping the spoon heavy with food, she would shout, curse, and say things that made me feel ashamed to be a husband, especially the fact that I couldn't afford whatever she wanted from the latest fashion in town. And when I couldn't bear listening to her anymore, I would leave the house and roam the compound. Outside, I would light a stick of cigarette and smoke till it was 2 am and the mosquitoes from the gutters containing excreta from broken toilet pipes became unbearable. By which time she would have gone to bed. Wrong. Damn wrong. She was waiting. Waiting for me to step right in so she would resume from where she stopped earlier.

"Look, *ehe*, Ndu bought his wife a gold necklace. When am I getting mine? The other day he bought her a nice shoe from a woman down the street, whose sister just came back from Paris. If you ever have a change of heart, I would be more than glad to walk you to the woman's place…" I would deliver a hard stare at Amaka until my chest started pounding as if it would explode. When I had finally given up on saying anything to her, I would mount my motorbike and head out. Ordeals such as the type I witnessed at home occurred regularly because of Ndu. The same Ndu who, from what every-one could see, took the bus to work every day and bought food at roadside *bukas* on credit. On several occasions the landlord had left notice of unpaid rents taped to the door of the one bedroom flat he rented with his wife. Yet he would return home and ignore the tape as if it was the last problem he had in the world. Then he would join me and other men at the *buka* down the road. Those times used to be evenings after work. We would talk and argue about the state of the nation, lament the soaring prices of fuel, the hike in food prices and the presence of the same old politicians whose roles in office seemed to be their birthright. Sometimes we even joked about how they probably reduced their ages so they escaped the retirement clause. How we came up with such conclusions did not matter. We lived in a country and time when what you saw or read gave you enough reason to believe what you heard. The newspapers did not fail us. *Nigerian Tide. The Guardian. Vanguard. New Nigerian.* They flashed news stories of the same juggernauts and their cabals. They were stories that showed how fame and power mated. Some of these men had been in government for the past four decades. When I grew tired of the stories, I gulped my last drop of palm wine and rushed home to another round of arguments with my wife.

The truth hurts. That was a fact. My wife was unsympathetic to my situation. Yesterday, just yesterday, she came to bed, nagging.

"Ndu bought his wife a nice shoe from a dealer on overseas wears," she said. I pretended I was asleep. The little I could do to save face, have peace of mind or, at least, escape another night of tantrums assaulting my ears. But I couldn't blame her. No. That would be wrong. At least I knew of women who did not depend on their husbands for gifts. Such women devised strategies with which they got whatever they wanted. Some accomplished their dreams by sleeping with men for money. Others of them, brilliant and hardworking and fired by the light of dignity and class, went to school, earned a degree, and wound up in top positions in oil companies or government offices in town. Men, as I hear, labored to have the hand of such women in marriage. Especially since, as I have heard, many of these women maintained they had absolutely no reason to depend on a man. But the truth, as some wino or sot once professed to me in a bar a long time ago, was that these women needed men at night for warmth and comfort. Yes, they may not agree wholeheartedly, but I knew that to be true.

And now my wife, the latest after my last divorce, appeared to be headed in the same direction as her predecessors. But thank God for Ndu's fate. When I heard two days later from the gossip in the street that he had taken two pills of Viagra before making love to his wife, I laughed till tears could no longer stroll down both sides of my cheek. The lesson was earned. That was my conclusion. And my poor wife. She never believed me. What did she know of working to earn a living? My father and mother had brought her to me from the village. They married her for me they said. I had no choice. Tradition called for obedience to parents. And so my distastes were only momentary asides swallowed to my own displeasure. It shall be well someday. That was all I promised myself.

Later, that afternoon, I bought groundnut from the boys who carried the little coffin-like wooden box placed over their heads while trekking in the sun. I sat on a cement pavement in the front yard, with the transistor radio I placed on the ground airing the latest news from BBC while my eyes feasted on local happenings from *The Nigerian Tide* newspaper. Happy? Yes, for once I was. I was happy that Ndu's generous and arrogant displays of possessions he bought from God knows-where, to impress his young wife, had stopped. But more importantly, I was mighty glad he would no longer be the catalyst for the unnecessary arguments my dear Amaka and I engaged in at home.

CHAPTER SEVEN

***

Boma's Wedding

Boma epitomized beauty in every respect. It was well known that suitors flooded her parents' home to intimate their intention to have her as wife. If she had any offside it remained the fact that she had no idea which of the men might suit her best as husband. Nor did she command the level of wisdom required to discern those who came for her hand merely because of her outward look and not for her character. She was reserved in nature, not given to wantonly bragging and publicizing of her suitors, but did comport herself wisely and remained a girl very much liked by the people of her community.

She stood an impressionable six feet one inch tall and her slender physique gave her away as someone slightly taller than she actually was. She walked with a lady-like swagger that appealed to men and took her time when speaking. The words did not rush out of her mouth. Instead they were controlled with eloquence and admirable diction. She spoke with a soft voice, one that left men trembling or all the more attentive. Perhaps if there was anything to the way she spoke it was that her appeal gave her away as one younger than her eighteen years of existence. This, as street gossip would have it, was what endeared her to the countless number pot-bellied wealthy men, many of whom were known to be politicians and titled traditional chiefs well into their fifties and sixties, who desired to add her to their coterie of wives. And it was by this same token that Chief D. M. showed up one day on campus and extended what seemed a rather fair approach to woo her, especially since his motorcade and American accent complemented his promise to spoil a young girl with money. She accepted his offer of friendship on a whim. Something her twenty-four-year-old university level boyfriend Wisdom, AKA Tiger, did not disapprove. He, for all his antics on campus as the firebrand and most dreaded cultist, needed money to defray cost of school fees and his upkeep. He wasn't going to depend on threatening students to pay him for protection, or obtaining from them, as students would put it.

Tiger was from a poor family. His fisherman father barely provided enough to feed his family of three wives and twenty children. Nor was his own mother's roadside fried bean cake and pap business going to be enough to see him through university. Hence the young man's decision to resort to a lifestyle of gangsterism, better known as cultism, whereby he and other young men his age were used by politicians to carry out rigging at election centers and serve as thugs at citywide events. And for all his underground work, Tiger enjoyed the benefit of his fine boy look. In fact there was the street gossip that spread like wildfire, that his mother must had come from a mixed parentage, because of his light complexion and almost silky and blonde hair, which gave him the so called pretty boy look. But those features of his meant little to Boma, especially when she was getting enough pocket money for new shoes, clothes and upkeep, after her tuition had been paid. No longer was she dependent on the pittance her charming Tiger used to provide. Besides her being with the chief was all Tiger's idea. He had planned it for his gain. And the sad thing was she didn't seem to comprehend his reasons but acceded to it, forgetting all about him in a heartbeat.

From boyfriend to bodyguard. That's what Tiger had become. Within a space of three months. Not once did he look her way for the momentary pleasure of a peck on the cheek or holding of hands in public. The chief was a brute who could order his other bodyguards to put him away for good, or threaten his family. And Tiger didn't want that. And so he did not sulk or keep a volte face when his once dear Boma placed her head on the chief's chest in public or rested against his shoulder in the backseat of the chief's Mercedes Benz, while Tiger, sitting in the passenger seat in front as the bodyguard for the day, ensured the driver followed the right routes to their destination. The music blasting off the CD player, a combination of Femi kuti, Tuface and P Square, soothed the mood for the two love birds representing two different generations. But there seemed to be something about the chief that Boma hadn't been able to place a finger on. Every time she tried to arrange for a meeting that would bring her mother and the chief together, her mother unexplainably fell ill and would need weeks to recover. In fact it was a mystery that had left the young girl devastated and all the more at a loss for words. She would stay in her one room flat off campus and cry in the company of friends, who would later comfort her without offering any idea of their own to help her salvage what appeared to be a mysterious ordeal. Then they would offer her chilled bottles of Fanta and chin chin, her favorite snack, to improve her mood. After which they would then slot in a DVD of the latest movie from one of the chief's imported collections for his bride to be. And they would watch attentively, breaking their focus every now and then to make sure they are not late for lectures.

The drive to lectures halls off Chobba Road could be hectic. Besides the chief had warned her to refrain from getting on okada motorbikes. So she knew if taking a taxi to class was her only option she had to leave early for lectures. Yet she loved taking her time in doing whatever she wanted, even if it resulted in her being late for lectures. It was purely a matter of habit. The elder chief knew this and had gotten fed up, but was afraid of losing her if he dragged on with his criticisms. The chief took care of Boma like he took care of his wives. The bi-weekly visit, all expenses paid for trip to the manicure and pedicure place off Aba Road, cost him nothing. Men are known to be hunters and a hunter hoping for a good catch knew nothing about giving up.

Besides being on guard to deflect competition, he had to be meticulous with matters of the heart when it came to dealing with women, especially a young girl in this case. So besides adhering to Boma's requests promptly, the chief took precaution to avoid being on her bad books. Money was never an issue that led to questions. Not when it concerned the chief and his bride to be. Most of the chief's friends, men his age, had warned him to be careful with young girls since their temperament could be suspect. Once the chief lost contact with Boma for two days after a violent rain storm hit the city and certain roads connecting streets in town were flooded, in addition to widespread power outage. He was distraught, but bore his grief with the confidence of a soldier who had been through life's battles with wooing women. By the third day he gave himself a good shave, slapped after shave cream on his face, put on his heavy beads and traditional attire, and off he went to Chobba with his driver. Moments after having his way into Boma's room he sat down quietly and carried out a cursory read of the *Ebony*, *Vogue*, and *Fashion* magazines lying on her desk. She offered him a plate of jollof rice and fried chicken after her friends had left that afternoon. The chief swallowed his pride and enjoyed the meal. Not a question was asked. He was beginning to be a good learner. Only men who honored patience got along well with women. But every now and then his ego pressed for answers as to why she did not call him in the past two days, but he blotted those worries from his memory and followed the dvd movie Boma had been watching. His heart was finally at peace. Yes, he was with her and she was not away from him. It was on this occasion he intimated the wedding proposal and presented before her the engagement ring. Her screaming out of excitement prompted Tiger to barge in through the door uninvited, only for him to realize all was well. Then he returned to the black Mercedes Benz parked across the road.

The arrangement for Boma's wedding to the chief commenced in earnest following a shopping spree in London. "My child, when is this man coming to see your father and I," asked Boma's mother, who was overjoyed that her daughter would be getting married. The joy of every mother. But the mystery remained: to whom? Rosemary, now fifty, had lost her vision in both eyes following a late diagnosis of Optin Neuritis. But she never felt out of place when it came to enjoying the good things of life. "Mommy, you will meet him soon. Don't worry!" Boma's reassurance seemed to work. Her mother trusted her daughter, especially when they both were looking forward to a wedding to a man who inherited acres of land rich in oil and who headed the nation's top fertilizer company. It was going to be only an aberration for anyone to doubt his spending potential. This was the case with men who possessed his kind of clout. They went for what they wanted and made the most out of the effort. "I will spoil you with money!" was a favorite line he often used in teasing Boma. Her grin moments later and silence in his arms gave him the reassurance he expected.

The day came. There had been nothing to suggest the unexpected. Chief D.M., elegant in his multicolored royal robe and hand fan made of feathers, stepped down from the backseat of his Hummer Jeep. His leather sandals, shiny and obviously not the kind sold in the local boutiques, and his wristwatch, a Movado with a distinct wristband, set eyes rolling. Whispers rose at every corner. Encomiums from attendees warmed his heart. Receptions of this magnitude made him think highly of himself. Of course, this was what royalty was made of him. Being admired by all and sundry. He soon sat on a leather armchair and gazed intently at the police officers watching while people jostled for space in the crowd. Feeling his bead while growing inpatient to set his eyes on his bride, Chief D.M. wondered what inadvertently delayed Boma and her family from arriving at the occasion.

Boma had never been to the chief's palace or his hometown for that matter. In fact this would be her first time to set foot on the kingdom that awaited their monarch's latest wife. And she had prepared for the occasion. For a young woman nearing nineteen, she had not known what to expect from such a luxurious event. All she knew was that she was getting married to a man who was almost her father's age. But that was not a problem at all. Her mother had approved of the wedding with a wave of the hand. Age was a matter of the heart, but wealth always guaranteed good health and comfort. "Remember my daughter! You are securing the future of your children when you marry a wealthy man, age notwithstanding." Her mother had never met the chief. In fact, Boma's wedding brought her mother home from the UK where she had spent the last twelve years. Rosemary had left the country when Boma was seven and had left her in the custody of her stepfather who raised her. The same stepfather who now was embroiled in a bitter feud with Boma's mother for allowing the young woman to marry a man thrice her age. Yet her mother remained adamant. If anything served as a lesson, it was her own life. Now almost blind, Rosemary would not wish the same fate she suffered for her young daughter.

"Who's this man you are getting married to? Where is he from? Have you met his people?" Rosemary's questions seemed to be endless. But the young woman was obsessed with her husband to be. The same man she called sugar, a nickname her own mother, Rosemary, called the chief when they both dated as college sweethearts two decades back. "Ah, how suddenly the world changes," stated Rosemary. "When we were growing up, we wanted to know all about a man before accepting his marriage proposal. But young women these days, eh!" Her daughter, craning her neck, looked up, and Rosemary chuckled. Then she reiterated her stance, reminding her daughter that she had made the right decision. After all, times were different! Young women married older men, just like older women married younger men.

The afternoon heat intensified. Royal maidens trudged through the occupied seats, refilling tumblers with orange juice and palm wine. The music was loud. Dancers from the village, a group of six ladies, swung their hips, their beads swaying, their feet moving. Not long after the entourage from Boma's family arrived. Then the band hired for the occasion resumed singing.

"Count your blessings, name them one by one," the choir of women and men from the local Episcopal Church sang, their white overalls glowing in the sun.

"Chudi, get the boys to roll the carpet, fast," the chief ordered, pausing to wipe his forehead with his handkerchief. When Boma stepped down from the backseat of the Mercedes wagon, jeers and claps exploded at every corner. The chief and his first wife stood up, clapping. They watched Boma tread softly on the red earth, her overflowing gown held from touching the ground by two young ladies.

Boma was resplendent in her attire. Her braids stretched all the way to her back. Her eyelashes covered by light colorings and her diamond earrings glittered impressively. Her high heels made her appear taller than her actual 6 feet 1inch height. Her red and black colored lace, hanging from her breast down, and her heavy neck beads and wrist beads, all red, matched perfectly. A woman assigned by the noble chief led the way, dropping petals of hibiscus on the ground just before Boma walked by.

Suddenly, just as Rosemary shook the chief's hand and he spoke, Rosemary appeared unsettled. There was something about the tone of her daughter's husband to be that she could not put a finger on. Rosemary prayed silently! No, it can't be, she whispered to herself. Then flashes of her past came flooding her mind. Images of twenty years ago. "God, don't let this be," said the hefty mother dressed in cream-colored lace and gold necklace whispered, holding tight to her daughter's hand. "Mother, are you all right," Boma said quietly. Rosemary was silent. By now an eerie quietness had descended on the crowd. The chief himself looked startled. The choir had stopped singing. It seemed time had stopped and every living thing had taken a break from existing. The picture was clear now. Rosemary knew the chief. She felt stiffness in her joints.

Sweat dribbled down her forehead. Yes. That voice, even after several years, remained the same. What more, he called Boma exactly the same name he called his beloved Rosemary, twenty years ago when she was his heartthrob: sugar. But the Donald Madu she knew more than twenty years ago had died in a car crash when he went on a business trip overseas. At least that was the account of the fatal crash his family offered the pregnant young woman who then carried his child. The heartbreaker that made Rosemary look elsewhere for another man to marry. Her suspicion was beginning to make sense now. But not after the wedding ceremony had been called off, with shouts of "get the ambulance" reverberating everywhere.

Two hours later, in a local clinic in the city, Rosemary would relay everything to her disappointed, yet anxious daughter, alone, in a hospital room. As she slowly drank from the bottle of Lucozade placed on a table next to her bed, Rosemary told Boma why it was perfectly all right that the ceremony had been called off. "Our ancestors forbid. Not while I am alive will you marry your own father."

CHAPTER EIGHT

***

Night Lesson

One night, my father and I stayed up late bagging used clothes we had planned to donate to the poor in our village when a sudden power outage compelled us to suspend our activity. I was left fuming as father tiptoed his way to the kitchen. I sat on the floor and mulled innumerable reasons why I should have traveled the day before in the company of mom and my sister Uju to the village, instead of facing another night of blackout when dad and I were the only tenants in the building. I had barely taken a break from these thoughts when dad returned to the living room. He handed me our rusty kerosene lantern and then scratched a matchstick. At the very moment the light flickered a bang floored the front door. Four men in ski mask stood before us. Two of them waved machetes menacingly, while the other two pointed their guns at us. "Shhh! No noise. Sit, on the floor!"

uttered the gang leader. I was frightened and almost shat my pants. Father

sat down quietly on the dusty floor. I was next. We watched in fear as the

men paced up and down the living room. One of the men flung open the

wardrobe and searched inside. The others packed and tied up our DVD

Player and small Sonny TV in a traveling bag. Next they circled the dining

table and fumbled through the mails. "Mumu, fool! Cut that envelope open

with your teeth if you can't use your fingernail," the gang leader snapped at

one of his men. The man addressed used a military knife instead and ended

up giving each torn envelope a fairly cursory inspection. I prayed fervently

that we wouldn't be hurt. But how wrong I was! As soon as they dropped

the bags of stolen items on the old sofa they entered the kitchen. What

could they be up to? I wondered. My curiosity increased the more till they

came back to the dining table with the pot of soup mom had made before

she left town. Using their hands, they dug the content, chewing on meat

and fish, spitting out bones and nodding in contentment. "Bros, this soup

na wahala!" I heard one of them declare. By this time the rain outside had

intensified. More drops drummed on the roof and I lamented the fact that our neighbor, an army Sergeant with a reputation for injecting fear into armed robbers in the area, had left the city for the village with his family earlier in the day. So this is what we get for being the only tenants in the compound, I pondered regretfully.

Time passed. Father and I watched irritably as the men entered the kitchen and returned to the dining table with the carton of Heineken dad had left on the kitchen floor. In a systematic display of solidarity, they uncapped the bottle with their teeth, gulped their beers, belched, and grinned. Father gazed at them disapprovingly, shaking his head. The thieves didn't seem to care about us. They mumbled and after drinking they circled us. The gang leader, a stout dwarf with a protruding forehead, cleared his throat and said: "Oga, do you have a gun or machete?" The smell of his alcohol breath left me feeling giddy. Father remained silent. "Organizer, leave this man alone," one of the men pleaded. The gang leader snapped a finger in dad's face, looked at him once, sighed and strode to the kitchen. His boys followed him.

They were loud and talked about the recent football game that Nigeria's men's national football team played against their South African opponents in Abuja and blamed the Europe based national team players for the outcome of the drab match which ended in a goalless draw. "Ye ye boys. Europe-based my yash! They couldn't even put a goal in the net," one of them griped. When they were done talking about football they criticized the new government policy that banned the operation of mopeds after 7:00 p.m., since the local police boss believed armed robbers operating in the night time took advantage of innocent civilians whom they robbed and then disappeared on motorbikes. "Enuh go better for the police commissioner and the governor, for putting sand for our food," one of the men said.

By this time the rainfall had stopped. They were still talking aloud. I smelled cigarette smoke and got nauseated, but pretty soon I got a relief as the night breeze strutting in from the space where once stood the front door cleared the air. Then the thieves returned to the living room. The gang leader laughed mockingly and stopped. "Did you guys hear that?" he asked, terrified. There was silence. Father was infuriated. I prayed silently that he wouldn't do something stupid, knowing the Christmas goat we bought from the market two days ago for fifty thousand naira had been kept in the storage. We watched the men tiptoe their way into the kitchen and soon there was pandemonium as they dragged the goat to the center of the living. The gang leader pointed at one of his boys and declared: "Ah, Dynamite, you will be the mama for this operation. Okay, get down." The man went on his knees first, then his hands. They placed the goat on his back like one would a baby on its mother's back, and then they emptied a cup full of salt in the goat's mouth. "Ah, Oga of the house, thank you for the Christmas gift," the gang leader said, staring at dad as he led his gang out through the back door.

Shortly after the robbers left dad and I sat up all night till the rain stopped dropping on the roof. The fear and confusion that dazed me while the thieves raided our home had left me by this time. Holding the kerosene lantern up, I noticed our living room was messy with clothes and envelopes torn open all over the place. After several moments of silence father reached for his work bag under the bed and brought out the old shoe polish container in which he stored snuff. Then he shoved a thumb full of snuff up his nostrils and seconds later sneezed noisily. I heard the rain dropping on the roof and said: "Daddy, it is still raining." He nodded and then shrugged in a manner that gave the feeling that his mind was elsewhere, occupied by things beyond what was happening outside. Then, in what struck me like a sudden twist in events, he heaved a sigh of relief and laid his hand on my shoulder. "Son," he said. "Bring me my handkerchief in the bathroom and the bucket of water under the sink." I stood up slowly from the edge of the bed, walked into the bathroom and came out moments later. "Sit here with me," dad said. His eyes were closed as though he had been sleeping while talking.

Outside we heard tires screeching and horns blaring.

Father adjusted his buttocks on the bed looking down at the bucket of murky, smelly water which had dead fish in it. He craned his neck to get a better view and then dipped his right hand in the bucket. I watched with puzzlement, intrigued by the prospect of witnessing firsthand what deservedly aroused his interest in a stinking bucket of water and dead fish

after all we had been through that night. Soon a grin formed on his mouth.

I watched his lips tremble as he wiped his hand dry on the bed sheet after

pulling out a plastic bag from the bucket. Then he cut open yet another

plastic bag he had retrieved from the same plastic bag. And there it was.

Bundles of rubber-strapped naira notes, crisp-looking. A strange silence

occupied the room after we heard a loud noise outside. We watched the

door, expectant of yet another robbery gang. But time passed and when we

saw no one walk in our apprehension died. We were safe. Then dad licked

his index finger and started counting the currency notes. "Aha" he said

when he was done and handed me a pen. Write down these numbers. Three

hundred thousand naira. I watched in folded arms, combing my thoughts

for a possible reason as why dad would take the risk of leaving such

amount of the money in the house. More so when we had just been

exposed to arm robbery attack. But dad would always be dad. Always

observant when others are engaged in loud talking. Was this why he

wouldn't say a word while the men in mask raided our rooms at will? Yes,

it was all beginning to make sense to me. After we both lifted and fixed the front door that night and then retired to bed I could hear dad snoring occasionally, exhausted. I pitied him and imagined how he coped with close to eighteen hours of driving, shuttling Aba and Port Harcourt roads to drop off travelers in his rusty Peugeot 504, all in the effort to support the family. Later that night, while I was asleep, dad woke me up and, looking in my tired eyes, he said: "Son, remember: remaining calm in the middle of a storm is never a sign of weakness." From that moment till the early hours of the following day, I never said a word again. Father made it clear and I understood it as clearly as he said it.

CHAPTER NINE

***

Changes

"Unbelievable." That was what I told myself as I sat there. Silent. Watching. Jude finally came home after twenty-two years in America. He came back a Pastor, a man of God at peace with preaching and praying for others. What an irony life is, I said to myself. Shaking my head, I went back forty three years and recalled my neighbor's eight year old son, who would spill rice from his mother's kitchen to a neighbor's barn, luring chickens that never made it back to their owner's barn once they entered his mother's kitchen. Yes, I stood there in disbelief. Life is full of wonders. Wonders that made us believe nothing is impossible. I sat there and remembered all the atrocities the young man had committed in his past until I realized he was standing before me, his eyes lighting with joy, his arms wide open.

"Auntie!" he shouted.

I gave him a hug. At least it wouldn't hurt to be good for one moment, I thought. Especially since I was meeting a man of God. Who knows? He might pray for my daughter Ego, the girl, my late husband, her father and I, her mother, had spent our lifetime's savings to send to university in America. And what did she do afterward? She forgot all about us, her father and myself. Instead we heard from Ntioro, our in-law's firstborn, a lecturer in a college in America, who had wanted to marry her when they were both secondary school kids in the country. He had met her once at the train station in Chicago.

"Auntie, it was one terribly cold day in December that we crossed paths-o," the young man had intoned.

We listened, arms folded, ears perking. He told us she was taking a boy whom he identified as her six-year-old son to school. He did not ask her if she were married or not. Americans, he said, were weary of people who stuck their nose in others business. Life! Such mystery it is, I said to myself, watching Jude speak. How proud his parents, Edet and Nkiru, must be. They sowed a seed before my eyes and today I am a witness to what it has bloomed into. What can I say? I knew my husband and I sowed ours too. I, like Aku, believed ours was going to sprout into something worth our encomiums and the encomiums of those who knew how disciplined and responsible we were. Looking at Jude now, I imagined asking God where my husband and I went wrong. That it rained on my roof to expose holes I had no prior knowledge of did not mean I was a careless home keeper.

So that afternoon I joined Edet and Nkiru to celebrate their son Jude's return home. Again, as I sat there feasting on the fried goat meat served with jollof rice and fried plantain and soft drinks, I recalled when Mabel, Edet's granny passed on. We all attended the lavish funeral at Eket.

People from Edet's place of work and those who knew him in the village arrived in large numbers. Handshakes, hugs, and well wishes lighted the occasion. But the highlight of the day, the one incident that silenced all and remained a childhood memory impossible to forget, was Jude's attempt at stealing the gold necklace in his dead granny's neck. Was it scolding? Was it spanking? Edet did it all to him and more, until Nkiru and some of the women from the family interceded on the helpless boy's behalf. Then they took him inside, away from the final events of the ceremony. I was shocked, at a loss for words, livid. So too was Aku. My husband was intolerant of undisciplined children. He could not stand a disobedient child's antics and often chided Edet, "Leave him to me for a week and you would not believe he is the same child of yours when I return him to you."

I recall a woman who sat behind us in disbelief, arms folded, asking Edet, "So what are you going to do to him to change him?"

Edet, in his usual way, chuckled, biting gently at the kola nut he brought out of the front pocket of his shirt, shaking his head. The woman got the message. Yes, she understood. Any man who has been trained in the Nigerian army and sent to war or military training was respected after he returned. People did not question the level of discipline of such a man. Such a man was not called a veteran of war for no reason. I myself knew what my dear husband could do to teach a child the way he should grow. After all, our daughter was an example. He never spanked her. All he did was sit her down and talk to her. And she could climb a mountain in a second if he ordered her to do so. And that was what I concluded he was going to do to Edet and Nkiru's son, the bad child who put his parents to shame.

Not long afterward, we were leaving that night after the funeral when we saw Jude kneeling on the concrete outside his father's bedroom door.

"Please, Edet, it's past nine. Let him go to bed. Don't forget he has to be in school before eight in the morning," Nkiru pleaded with her husband.

That was how Jude escaped his father's attempt to straighten him up. What a bad boy he was as a child.

I was still thinking of him and his horrible childhood when I heard someone ask him of Ejike, the son of the man we used to refer to as *The Politician.*

"Ejike died," Jude said quietly, unfolding in mixture of sadness and pain.

"Chei!" exclaimed the elderly man who had asked him about his secondary school mate and distant cousin's son. After shrugging and shaking his head, the same man looked Jude in the face and said: "My son, what happened?"

Jude narrated one story after another until he got to the one dealing with Ejike being a cab driver in Chicago. One night, he carried on, blinking, coughing to clear his throat, Ejike never returned to the apartment he rented in the same building where they all used to live on the city's North side. They were all worried and called the police two days later to alert them of their good friend's disappearance, only for them to hear the unexpected, on the third day, that he had been shot twice in the head two nights before. A victim of attempted robbery, the police would later confirm. Jude stopped talking, and wiped his eyes with his handkerchief. Then, adjusting his glasses, he stared the elder in the face and said: "Uncle Udo, I cannot say anymore. I think it is only proper for his father and mother to tell you what happened next, or whatever you wish to know about their son."

By this time, more visitors were entering and leaving Edet and Nkiru's house. The sun seemed like one gigantic orange hanging in the blue sky. The air was hot, with humidity at an unbearable high. I stood up, trusting my cane, holding it firmly. Then I walked outside, where I met Nkiru.

"Ah, Jane, are you leaving already?" she said, her eyes full of the same excitement I had been accustomed to for the past forty-three years we have known each other.

I nodded.

She shrugged and said: "Well, okay. So when do we see you again?" I paused momentarily, looked up, then down.

"Aku is still inside with Edet. As for me, I shall be back to see you and the family after church on Sunday. Please tell Edet I am proud of Jude," I said.

I could see the waves of pride in Nkiru's eyes. For a moment I wanted to tell her of my own daughter and the pain I felt, but the lump in my throat betrayed me. Instead, not knowing she herself had received a letter written by my daughter delivered by their son, I shook her hand, hugged her, let go and headed in the direction of the bus stop, wiping my eyes continuously, after a speeding bus had me covered in a cloud of dust.

Two days later, while sitting in Nkiru and Edet's living room, I had the opportunity to see my own daughter's writing, courtesy of the letter she wrote to her favorite Auntie Nkiru. The fact that I stopped short of the last sentence in the concluding paragraph was not what prompted my refusal to carry on. There was actually more to it. Yes. Looking back now, it must have been the burden of guilt, for her only reference to me, her mother, remained those three words we often find difficult to say: I love you. And even after I went home, I imagined her father reading the same letter, his wet eyes holding the same wave of excitement found in my eyes as I silently mull over our daughter's heartfelt words.

CHAPTER TEN

***

The Mysterious Tire Thief

Chico lay still in bed, snoring away face up that morning when he was awakened by loud knocks on the door. Awoke from a deep sleep, having returned home at about 3 a.m., his muscles aching, he reached for the alarm clock on the table supporting the 12" oscillating table fan, peeked at the time, sighed and went back to sleep. Then another round of knocks followed. The bed creaking, he rolled off and grabbed a T-shirt.

"Yes!" he shouted in an unreal voice.

"Open, it's me, Countryman," answered the sharp male voice.

Realizing it was his landlord, he pretended to be someone else, for he owed rent for the past two months. "Chico is not here. Please, come back some other time."

"Open, Chico," repeated the voice. "I know you are inside."

Inside, Chico meditated in silence as he tiptoed here and there. Then he wondered what to do to get rid of the unwanted disturbance. With his heart beating like a drum marshalled by multiple palms, he said, "Go away, Countryman. I don't have your rent today."   More knocks followed, but Chico remained silent.

"Open, Chico. Dem don carry your car tire."

"Shut up!" shouted Chico, his voice sounding more like him. "You want me to open the door so you can use another police warrant to evict me, eh?"

"I see. Maybe you can drive your car to work without tire, eh," intoned his landlord.

Chico kept mum. Moments later the great cry of 'Thief! Thief! Thief-oo!' grew outside as a crowd drew past his apartment. Countryman was right, thought Chico. He scrambled under the bed and grabbed his machete. It was now about 6.50 a.m. The door opened. Countryman was standing outside, holding a kitchen knife. "Please don't harm me," he cried, clearing the way for a desperate Chico.

"Where is the thief?" shouted Chico. He eyes were wide open. He had a short beard scattered over his chin. Chewing a kola nut, he watched the now distant crowd set out in the direction down the road. He turned to Countryman.

"Foolish man," cursed Countryman. "You don't believe me, eh. Thought I was here for the debt you owe me. You better go get your tire so you don't get sacked at work." Chico changed his countenance and sought a quick explanation for the event that had unfolded. Countryman intimated that as many as four cars had been robbed of tires in the early hours of the morning, and that people in the street were convinced the last car robbed was his. He rushed to the front of the gate and confirmed with one angry gaze that it was indeed true, as his boss's black Mercedes Benz was missing a front tire. All the robberies led to a street urchin and ruffian, midget, John Blaze.

"Enough of your story!" shouted Chico. "Where is he?"

Countryman was going to speak when more armed youths from the neighborhood went past the apartment and pushed in the direction of the crowd. One of the men had tripped over a stone and fell. As he stood up Chico held him by the hand and demanded to know what was going on. "So you haven't heard, eh? That idiot Blaze stole your tire!" Chico looked down, then skywards, raving in anger. When he lowered his chin, the youth was gone. So too was Countryman, who had joined the chase.

Farther down the road, the sun was hiding its orange face up in the heavens. Anger tearing him apart, Chico battled to keep his focus as he meditated silently on what he would do if he caught up with the robber. His toes hurt for he had no shoes on. Then he started running in the direction of the crowd. But halfway down the road, he fell after his big toe struck a stone. With his eyes closed, teeth firmly clutched together and, holding his foot with both hands, he sat down on the red soil, shaking his head as teardrops dribbled down his cheek. Moments later, Countryman, who had abandoned the chase to look for Chico, found him wounded and in pains. "Lazy boy," he said. "Get up and be a man. I know you can't let that idiot have a fun day on your tire. Ha! Remember, that tire is your means of livelihood."

Chico looked up, picked up his machete and dragged the wounded foot, limping as he went after the crowd. Countryman was ahead of him, but every now and then he turned to see if Chico was catching up with the chase. His mind was clouded with the money Chico owed him. More people joined the chase from different directions. The chase took the crowd through a bush path. The music of birds in the bush was alive, and occasionally a few flew over the crowd, disappearing in different directions. By this time Chico's mind became crowded with weary voices. The voices were engaged in laughter. Occasionally one voice took precedence over the others and shouted "my money, my money! You better get your tire so you can pay your debt to me!"

Soon the short spell of sunshine gave way to a drizzle. But that did not stop the chase. Ahead, the midget stopped to measure the distance between his destination and his followers. The discovery spelt doom for they were closing in. Eyes wide open, holding the tire with his stubby fingers, he picked up speed, heading in the direction of the river. He stood about four feet seven inches with large feet the size of swim fins. The crowd followed. On both sides of the road were trees. The drizzle had stopped and the sky was now a beauty of radiant blue. The crowd increased as people from other streets and short cuts had joined the raid. Further down, the image of the thief seemed to diminish in size as he pushed for the river ahead. The cocks were crowing repeatedly as though engaged in a crowing contest, signaling the break of a new day. But it wasn't anything like a new day the like of which Chico would have wished for. He had been thinking of his job all along. The stolen tire belonged to the New African Soft Drink Company where he had just been hired and appointed head driver to the director of city's branch office. He had driven the car home instead of packing it at his boss's home as was company policy, without his boss's approval. And the event of the moment seemed headed for his exposure. Realizing only the recovery of the tire will erase his mounting anxiety, he stood still for a moment and bit his lower lip as the crowd closed in on the thief who was now faced with nowhere to run to.

'Thief Thief!' the cry mounted in the heat. Chico squinted as he got a closer view of the robber.

Ahead, down by the river, he noticed a little image bouncing with a ring-like object over its head. Realizing that the midget was approaching the river, fear engulfed Chico. He tried to think of a convincing excuse not to lose his job if he reported the theft to his boss later in the day, but abandoned the thought quickly.

Soon he arrived by the river, gasping. He went in front of the crowd and waved. There was silence. Then he turned to the midget. They eyed each other. The crowd had formed a ring round both men by this time.

'Everybody step back!' ordered Chico.

The roar ceased. Chico cleared his throat and looked piercingly into the midget's eyes. The midget turned to look at the river and then back at Chico. The crowd watched with anticipation, Chico declared 'You dis thief, you go die today!' He grabbed the midget by the head. The midget dropped the tire and delivered a kick. Chico moved back swiftly. The crowd hovered. Then, from every direction, fists, sticks, and stones descended on the midget. He went down on his knees, covering his face with his stubby fingers. When the crowd heard the sound of a powerboat engine starting up from afar, they abandoned the attacks and shifted their attention to the boat. Then the midget stood still, with the expression on his face suddenly changing. His nose was wide open. He was now holding a long dagger and reached for Chico's rib side. 'Cut e no go enter!' Chico shouted, daring the midget to take his chance and inferring not even a stab would penetrate his skin. Quickly, the midget dropped the knife and meandered between the crowd. How he got through the sea of legs successfully remained a mystery, with Chico holding his car tire and watching in terror like the rest of the crowd, as the midget dived into the water, and disappeared. A broad smiled crossed Chico's face and not long after, an angry youth went past him and attempted a dive into the river. "Don't follow him," someone cautioned with a soft voice from afar. When the crowd turned back to look at the speaker they realized it was an old woman holding a walking stick. Suddenly the angry youth gave up his intent. Everybody was silent. Many studied the water as the steel-like glitter had transformed into a peaceful tide. The smell of decaying dead animals and oil was now strong in the air. No trace of the midget was visible. Vultures at midair flapped their large wings, reaching for the waters but returned to the sky without facing any visible obstacle. The old woman was now standing close to the crowd. How she got close to them so soon was beyond their comprehension. She was pale and wore a white wrapper covering from her chest down. The crowd stared at her in dismay. 'Go home children,' she said. 'It is not everything the eyes see that they really see. The water is not meant for all. The land turtle cannot claim to belong to the water because the sea turtle belongs to it too. He dived into the water, right? Now look carefully. Are you able to trace him?' There was a prolonged silence. Then, gradually, the crowd dispersed as people pushed in different directions.

Praise for Okoro's fiction:

I like the way Okoro's stories gives us glimpses into everyday occurrences in a manner that is at once accessible and profound.

--Benjamin Kwakye
Double Commonwealth Book Prize for Fiction-Winner

These stories portray life as instances of change under a canopy of love, avarice, determination, redemption, and triumph. They are all vignettes of life in certain realistic and ephemeral ways. [Okoro] portrays realism and illusion as two sides of a coin which inevitably propel us into fantasy, and awareness. The stories have a certain speed. They seem to move and confront us with certain vagaries of life. We enjoy these vagaries even when they occur unexpectedly as in "The Cross Bearer", where we find out that the person falsely accused of impregnating a girl was finally released when the real culprit was discovered. In "Boma's Wedding" the plight of someone unknowingly falling in love and wanting to marry her own father becomes a kind of puzzle, a certain tragedy of errors, so to speak. The fact that in most of the stories the environment is Port Harcourt Nigeria makes it homely for Nigerian readership. The reader of these short stories will also enjoy the candor, the humor and the wit inherent in them, particularly when the story stops to delve into a dream sequence and finally back into the actual story mode. The metaphorical intention of the author agrees with the literary symbolism of each short story. This is a delight.

--Oladipo Kalejaiye, PhD
Head of Department, Theater Art & Culture,
Lead City University, Ibadan, Nigeria

Dike Okoro's awards include the Sam Walton Fellowship and an honorable mention for the Iliad Literary Award. His fictional work and nonfiction have appeared in *HackWriters* (Canada), *World Literature*

Today, *Eclectica*, and elsewhere. He is the editor of *Speaking for the Generations: Contemporary Short Stories from Africa* (Trenton: Africa World Press, 2010). He teaches at Northwestern University, Chicago.

Printed in the United States
By Bookmasters